EL DORADO COUNTY LIBRARY

3 1738 00968 0297

D0384782

This Book Donated to
the Children of Placerville by
Mr. Gordon Purdy
Who Loved Children and
Books in That Order -
Usually.

EL DORADO COUNTY LIBRARY
345 FAIR LANE
PLACERVILLE, CA 95667

Little Patriot Press

Woodrow
The White House Mouse

El Dorado County Library
345 Fair Lane
Placerville, CA 95667

By Peter W. Barnes and Cheryl Shaw Barnes

Text copyright © 2012 by Peter W. Barnes
Jacket art and interior illustrations copyright © 2012 by Cheryl Shaw Barnes

All rights reserved. No part of this publication may be reproduced or transmitted in any form
or by any means electronic or mechanical, including photocopy, recording, or any information
storage and retrieval system now known or to be invented, without permission in writing from
the publisher, except by a reviewer who wishes to quote brief passages in connection with a
review written for inclusion in a magazine, newspaper, broadcast, or on a website.

Cataloging-in-Publication data on file with the Library of Congress
ISBN 978-1-59698-788-3

Published in the United States by
Little Patriot Press
an imprint of Regnery Publishing, Inc.
One Massachusetts Avenue, NW
Washington, DC 20001
www.Regnery.com

Manufactured in the United States of America
10 9 8 7 6 5 4 3 2 1

Books are available in quantity for promotional or premium use.
For information on discounts and terms write to
Director of Special Sales, Regnery Publishing, Inc.,
One Massachusetts Avenue, NW, Washington, DC, 20001, or call 202-216-0600.

Distributed to the trade by
Perseus Distribution
387 Park Avenue South
New York, NY 10016

We dedicate this book

to all the presidents,
first ladies, and their families,
and to all the men and women who have served
in the White House and executive branch—
thank you for your hard work and public service.
It is also dedicated to one of those women
in particular, Nancy Fleetwood Miller:
a special thank you for being a great
"campaign manager"—without you,
Woodrow would never have made it to the Oval Office!

—P.W.B. and C.S.B.

★ ★ ★

Find the **Presidential Seal** hidden in each illustration.

Every four years, like the rest of us do,
The mice of the nation elect someone, too,
To live in Washington's grandest old house,
A leader respected—a president mouse!

Woodrow G. Washingtail won the last vote.
"A mouse Yankee Doodle!" the newspapers wrote.
So good and so brave, and smart, if you please—
His favorite food? Why, American cheese!

So on a cold winter's day, with most solemn respect,
Two presidents swore to preserve and protect
Our nation, our freedoms, our flag, see it wave—
Our land of the free and our home of the brave.

The White House was lit, floor to roof, wall to wall,
For the beautiful, splendid Inaugural Ball.

Soon Woodrow arrived, with his First Lady, Bess,
And their children in tow—about eight, more or less.

There were Truman and Franklin, their two oldest sons,
And Quentin and Kermit, the mischievous ones,

SAY . . . . . .
CHEESE . . . . .

And Dolley and Millie, and the twins, George and Art
(not even their classmates could tell them apart).

The State Room was filled with good will and good cheer—
The mouse children watched from the great chandelier.
It was going quite well, until George, with a whoop,
Slipped and landed—ker-splash—in a senator's soup!

The president has a big job, you'll agree—
Many places to go, many people to see.

RIGHT NOW

In the great Oval Office, he does all his thinkin'—
And Woodrow, they say, is as smart as Abe Lincoln!

CAMPAIGNER'S GUIDE TO ADVANCED BABY KISSING

RUBBER CHICKEN RECIPES

KEEPING POLITICAL PROMISES By Senator I. BRAKUM DALEY

SHAKE A MILLION HANDS & KEEP SMILING

PRESIDENTIAL WIT

NEW HAMPSHIRE VACATION GUIDE

DUCKEM & DODGER'S PRESS CONFERENCE HANDBOOK

OF MEN AND MICE BY JOHN MOUSEBECK

FAMOUS SPEECHES OF SIR WINSTON CHURCHMOUSE

The president mouse has a desk on the shelf,
Where he works with his helpers or just by himself.
Our grand Constitution keeps a president busy—
So many assignments, a mouse could get dizzy!

The primary job of
    the president mouse
Is working with Congress,
    the Senate and House,
On making new laws
    for the good of the nation—
Health, peace, and justice
    for the whole population!

Approved _Woodrow G. Washingtail_ _____

Vetoed _____

Approved _____

Vetoed _Woodrow G. Washingtail_ _____

The president is required to study each "bill"
That Congress delivers from Capitol Hill.
If he signs it, a bill becomes law—it's approved.
If he gives it a "veto," it's rejected, removed.

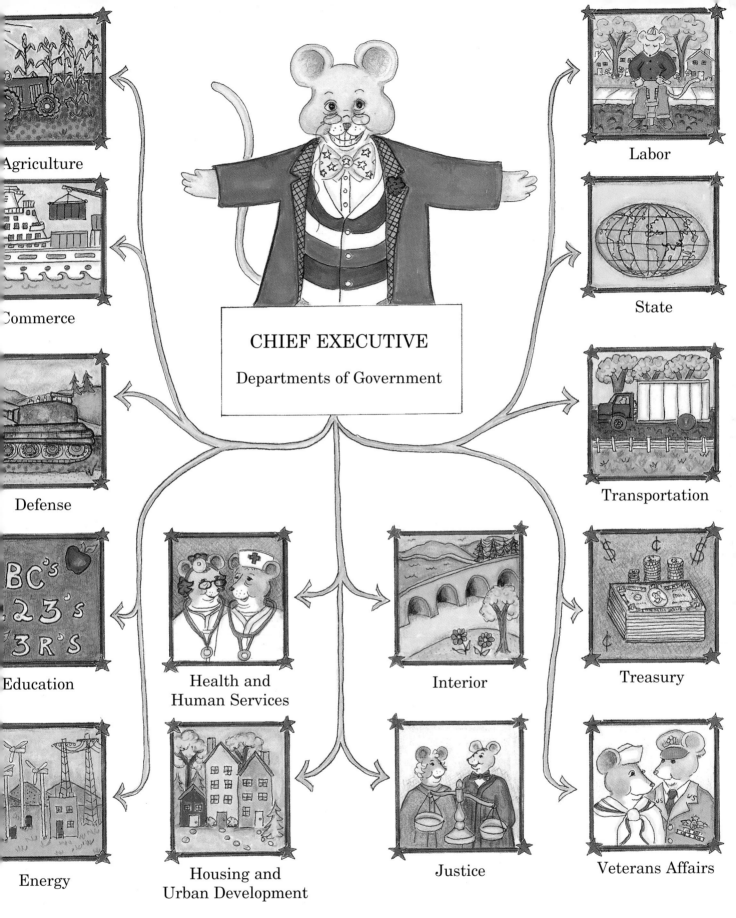

Agriculture

Commerce

Defense

Education

Energy

Labor

State

Transportation

Treasury

Health and
Human Services

Interior

Housing and
Urban Development

Justice

Veterans Affairs

He's the "Chief Executive," which means he's in charge
Of government departments, the small and the large.
Government departments include Transportation,
Justice and Labor—and, of course, Education.

He is also "Commander in Chief," and that means
The Army and Navy, Air Force and Marines
Report to the president as boss, the "Big Cheese"—
On this, every soldier and sailor agrees!

The president regularly talks with and greets
The leaders from foreign countries he meets.
In this job, the president is our "Head of State"
When handling foreign affairs, small and great.

But the president also gets time out to play—
Every Easter, for instance, is egg-rolling day!
There are orange eggs, yellow eggs—purple eggs, too!
There are even some eggs colored red, white, and blue!

Inside the White House,
 there's also more fun
For Woodrow, his family,
 and most everyone!
The East Room is used
 for artistic events,
Like concerts and shows
 for mouse ladies and gents!

One night, Millie dreamed that on one special day
She might, if she practiced, dance an East Room ballet.
She'd be joined by the famous Marine Mouse Quartet
For her flawless finale, a fine pirouette.

The Red Room and Green Room are not side by side,
But they're wonderful places for children to hide.
When they play hide and seek, and Woodrow is seeking,
He finds them so fast—could it be that he's peeking?

The Blue Room at Christmas is decked to the ceiling.
The fire is roaring—the children, all squealing,

Excited that Christmas is once again here,
To share with our loved ones and those we hold dear.

And as he nodded to sleep,
   the good president mouse
Was thankful for family
   and country (and house!).
"It's all so wonderful,"
   was his happy reflection,
"That a fellow just might
   want to seek re-election!"

The Presidency

After the United States became independent from England in 1783, the Founding Fathers did not want another king, with unchecked power, to run the young country. So in the Constitution they divided power among three equal branches of government: the legislative (Congress), the judicial (Supreme Court), and the executive (president). The idea was to create a system of checks and balances, with no one branch dominating the other. To make changes and get things done, there had to be general agreement among all three.

The Constitution says that to be president, a person has to be at least 35 years old and a natural-born American citizen. The president is elected every four years. He is allowed to serve only two four-year terms. The Constitution gives the president specific powers. As Chief Executive, he runs the government, enforcing laws and directing the many departments and agencies that implement them. He is also required to work with Congress on creating laws; not only does he make his own proposals for legislation, he must approve or reject (veto) proposed laws after they have passed Congress. Each year, the president goes to Congress to give the State of the Union address, a "report card" on the nation, to let everyone know how the country is doing. He also usually uses the address to propose his goals for the nation in the year ahead.

The president not only works with Congress, he also works with leaders of other countries, negotiating treaties and agreements on trade, keeping peace, and dealing with other issues of mutual interest. In this capacity, the president acts as our Head of State. As Head of State, he is also expected to be America's biggest cheerleader, upholding its traditions, dedicating monuments, presenting awards, and participating in other ceremonial functions at home and abroad. Finally, the Constitution says the president is the Commander in Chief of the nation's military: the Army, Navy, Air Force, Marines, and Coast Guard.

The Tail End
Resources for Parents and Teachers

Fun Facts about Presidents

James Madison, the 4th president, was also the smallest at five feet, four inches tall and less than 100 pounds. The tallest president was the 16th, Abraham Lincoln, who stood six feet, four inches tall. The heaviest was the 27th, William Howard Taft, who was six feet, two inches tall and weighed more than 300 pounds. The president with the most children was the 10th, John Tyler, with 15. The oldest elected to the office was the 40th, Ronald Reagan, who was 69 when he took office. The youngest elected was the 35th, John F. Kennedy, who was 43. Teddy Roosevelt, the 26th, was the youngest unelected president; as vice president, he succeeded to the office at the age of 41 upon the death of William McKinley in 1901. The president who served the shortest term was the 9th, William Henry Harrison, who died of pneumonia a month after his inauguration. The longest-serving president was the 32nd, Franklin Roosevelt, who served just over 12 years.

The White House

When the Founding Fathers prepared their plans for a new federal city on the Potomac River, they included an Executive Mansion for the president. George Washington chose the site on which the mansion was built. In 1792, an Irish-born architect, James Hoban, won a competition to design it. In 1800, while it was still under construction, President John Adams moved in—presumably along with the first White House mice.

The mansion underwent many changes through the years. It had to be rebuilt after the War of 1812 (the British burned it). The south portico was added in 1824, and the north portico in 1830. The West Wing

The Tail End
Resources for Parents and Teachers

was added in the early 1900s; the East Wing was constructed during World War II and included the first White House movie theater. A third floor was added to the main structure in 1927. During the Truman administration, the house went through a major renovation.

Over the years, the building was called the President's House and the Executive Mansion. In 1901, Teddy Roosevelt officially changed the name to the White House.

★ ★ ★

Of the building's more than 100 rooms, several of the most famous are featured in this book. The State Room is used for the president's official dinners. The East Room—the largest room—is used for entertaining, concerts, dances, press conferences, and more. The Red Room serves as a parlor, as does the Green Room. The Blue Room is the main reception room. The Oval Office is where the president conducts official business.

In many of this book's illustrations, Cheryl Barnes has recreated the actual furnishings and decorations of those rooms. In the Oval Office illustration, for example, the president is seated at the Resolute Desk, which was made from the oak timbers of the British ship *Resolute*. The desk was given as a gift to President Hayes by Queen Victoria in 1880, after the stranded ship was rescued by American whalers in the Arctic and returned to England.

Woodrow's First Lady and children have familiar names. Bess is named for Bess Truman. Woodrow's oldest son, Truman, is named for President Truman. Franklin is named for President Franklin Roosevelt. Quentin and Kermit were the names of two of

The Tail End
Resources for Parents and Teachers

the sons of Teddy Roosevelt. Dolley is named for Dolley Madison, First Lady to James Madison. Millie is the name of a Springer Spaniel owned by President George Bush. George is named for George Washington, and Art, for President Chester A. Arthur.

★ ★ ★

Anyone who has visited the Smithsonian Institution may recognize one of Bess's dresses in the book. At the Inaugural Ball, she is wearing the gown worn by Mamie Eisenhower for the first inaugural celebration for her husband, President Dwight D. Eisenhower, in 1953. It has 4,000 rhinestones and its pale pink color was soon known as "Mamie Pink." The dress is in the Smithsonian's collection of First Ladies' gowns.

★ ★ ★

The annual Easter Egg Roll noted in the book was originally held at the Capitol. It moved to the White House in 1878, when President Hayes and his wife, Lucy, opened the South Lawn for the event. It is always held on the Monday after Easter.

★ ★ ★

For more information on the White House, contact or visit the White House Historical Association online at http://www.whha.org.

Acknowledgments

We want to thank Larry Householder,
for all his invaluable help and guidance;
Jim Miller, for letting Nancy out to play
all those early mornings and late nights;
Jim and Carole Kuhn, for the use of their great pictures;
Jill Parker, and Meg and Stephen Upton,
for being great Easter egg rollers;
our families, for their love and support;
and our two wonderful daughters,
Maggie and Kate, for their patience.

—P.W.B. and C.S.B.

Appreciation

We would especially like to thank
Nancy Fleetwood Miller, who opened
doors and made introductions for us.
She was Director of Congressional Affairs,
U.S. Department of Transportation, during
the Reagan administration and then served
as Special Assistant to President George H. W. Bush
at the White House. She and her husband Jim
have two daughters and live in Alexandria, Virginia.

—P.W.B. and C.S.B.

JAN 0 3 201

JAN 0 3 2015